Elephant's Lunch

Written by Kate Walker
Illustrated by Ann James

An easy-to-read SOLO
for beginning readers

Omnibus Books
A.C.N. 000 614 577
52 Fullarton Road, Norwood, South Australia 5067
part of the SCHOLASTIC GROUP
Sydney · Auckland · New York · Toronto · London
www.scholastic.com.au

First published 1998
Reprinted 1999 (twice), 2000

Text copyright © Kate Walker 1998
Illustrations copyright © Ann James 1998

Cover design by Lyn Mitchell
Typeset by Clinton Ellicott, MoBros, Adelaide
Printed and bound by Hyde Park Press, Adelaide

National Library of Australia Cataloguing-in-Publication entry
Walker, Kate, 1950 Jan 10–   .
Elephant's lunch.
ISBN 1 86291 374 9.
I. James, Ann. II. Title. (Series: Solos
(Norwood, S. Aust.)).

A823.3

An earlier version of *Elephant's Lunch* was published in *The Macquarie
Bedtime Story Book* (Macquarie Library, Sydney, 1987)

For my grandmother – K.W.

For Leonie Gaff and Gang – A.J.

Chapter 1

Clara stared into her school bag. She frowned.

"Are you sure you've given me enough lunch?" she asked her mother.

"Enough lunch!" her mother said. "You've got four peanut butter sandwiches, six bananas, a piece of chocolate cake and an apple pie!"

"But I'll be at school all day,"
Clara said, "and I get *awfully*
hungry."

"You won't get hungry," said her mother. "You couldn't possibly get hungry! You've got enough lunch in there to fill an elephant. Now off we go."

Chapter 2

Clara and her mother walked down to the wharf to wait for the ferry boat.

While her mother talked to other people there, Clara went to talk to the elephant she'd seen waiting outside.

He was big and grey, with soft
little eyes.

"Hello," Clara said.
The elephant blinked, and looked
away across the water.

Clara looked too. She saw tug-
boats and tankers and yachts. But
no ferry boat.

"Are you waiting for the ferry
too?" she asked.

The elephant said nothing.

"Once I waited for the ferry," Clara said, "and it was late, and I got *awfully* hungry. So hungry that my tummy growled and made a big pain. I hope you're not hungry, because you've got a really big tummy and you'd get an *awfully* big terrible pain."

Again the elephant said nothing.
But Clara saw that his ears hung
low.

Chapter 3

Clara knew all about waiting for ferries and how hungry it made you. More hungry than waiting for buses, or waiting for traffic lights to change.

Poor elephant.

Just in case the ferry was late,
he should have something to eat.

Clara opened her school bag. Elephants liked peanuts, everyone knew that.

She took a peanut butter
sandwich and offered it to him.

The elephant just blinked.

"Yummy, peanut butter!" Clara said, and rubbed her tummy.

The elephant blinked again. He didn't understand.

YUM! YUM! YUM!

Chapter 4

To show the elephant what she meant, Clara ate the first sandwich herself, making loud munching noises.

Then she held out the second
sandwich. But the elephant blinked
as before and didn't say a word.

Maybe it's monkeys that like peanuts, Clara thought.

She ate the second sandwich, saying, "Mmm! Mmm!" and rolling her eyes.

Still the elephant didn't seem to understand.

Clara ate the third sandwich and licked her lips. "Mmmmmmmm!" she said.

The elephant raised his trunk and scratched his ear.

Maybe he isn't very smart, Clara
thought.

She held out the fourth sandwich and said, "If you don't eat this last yummy peanut butter sandwich, I will!"

The elephant said nothing, just let his trunk sag.

"This is your last chance." Clara raised the sandwich to her mouth.

"And this is your second-last chance." She opened her mouth wide.

"And this is your third-last chance." She put the sandwich in her mouth.

The elephant looked away.
And the last peanut butter sandwich was gone.

Chapter 5

Clara looked across the water. There were speedboats and row-boats and a catamaran. But no ferry boat.

"You may not know this," Clara said to the elephant, "but some ferry boats are so late they don't come at all. You'd get an *awfully* big pain in your tummy then."

The elephant's shoulders drooped.

He's starting to understand now, Clara thought.

She opened her bag and took out six bananas.

He was a very big elephant. He could eat them all. So she peeled them and laid them on the seat beside him.

But the elephant just sat and stared across the water.

Perhaps it's gorillas who like bananas, Clara thought.

Now they were peeled, someone had to eat them. So Clara did.

"You're the fussiest animal I ever met," she told the elephant. "And you'll be sorry when your ferry doesn't come and you're so hungry that you get a terrible big pain."

Chapter 6

Clara looked in her school bag once more. "I suppose you like chocolate cake?" she said.

Everyone in the whole world liked chocolate cake! Mothers and fathers, mice and parrots, cats and dogs.

Clara looked across the water.
She could see a paddle boat and
some kayaks. But no ferry boat.

"All right then," she said. "I'll share my chocolate cake with you."

She broke the cake in two, and put one piece on the seat beside the elephant.

She started to put the other piece back in her bag. But she had to have just one little bite.

Then another.
Then just one more.
Now there was only one bite left.
No use putting that little bit away!

Clara popped it into her mouth.

Then she heard *Toot! Toot!.*
It was the ferry. The elephant
wouldn't go hungry after all.

Chapter 7

Clara snatched up the elephant's piece of cake, thinking of all the other people in the world who liked chocolate too. Grandmas and grandpas, big sisters, little brothers, teachers, police – everyone!

Toot! The ferry pulled into the wharf. And Clara saw that the elephant had gone. And so had the piece of chocolate cake she'd had in her hand.

Now all she had left for a whole day's lunch was one not-very-big apple pie.

"Oh dear," Clara said to herself. "I'm going to get *awfully* hungry. Just like the time I waited for a ferry and it didn't come. My tummy will growl at me and make a pain."

Chapter 8

Clara acted quickly.

She gobbled down the apple pie to make her school bag light and told her mother: "Quick, we've got to go home and get some more lunch."

She held open her empty bag.
Her mother stared in shock.

"Clara!" she said. "What happened
to the lunch I gave you?"

"I ate it," Clara said. "I had to. There was this elephant, see, waiting for the ferry, and ..."

"It was an elephant today," her mother said.

"That's right, a big one," said Clara.

"Not a gorilla?" said her mother. "No," said Clara. "The gorilla was yesterday."

"And not a monkey?" her mother said.

"Don't you remember?" said Clara. "I met the monkey the day before."

Her mother shook her head. "Clara, I don't know where you put all this food," she said.

"In my tummy, of course," said Clara, "so it won't growl and make a pain."

"Well, I hate to say this," said her mother, "but, Clara, you eat like an elephant."

"That isn't true!" said Clara. "I happen to know that elephants don't eat very much at all."

And neither do camels – as Clara found out on her way to school the very next day!

Kate Walker

Elephants are my favourite animal, perhaps because the very first chapter book I ever read was about a boy who made friends with a jungle elephant. The elephant helped him, and he helped the elephant. They were best friends. After that I read every elephant book the library had.

Or maybe I like elephants because they remind me of my grandmother. She was a big lady, with lots of wrinkles and little kind eyes, and she swayed from side to side as she walked. Because it might have hurt her feelings, I never told her she reminded me of an elephant – but she did!

Ann James

I had great fun doing the illustrations for this book. I think it's a lovely idea to have an elephant to chat to while you are waiting for the ferry to arrive.

When I'm waiting for a ferry or a tram or a train I like to look at everything around me. Most of all I like to watch people and animals. Sometimes I make up stories in my head about them – where they live, why they look happy or sad.

I often get hungry when I'm waiting, too, but no one has ever shared their lunch with me – yet!